Sam's Wild West CHRISTMAS

Nancy Antle

PICTURES BY

S. D. Schindler

DIAL BOOKS FOR YOUNG READERS

NEW YORK

*For my son, Ben, whose sense of
humor keeps me going*
N. A.

Published by Dial Books for Young Readers
A division of Penguin Putnam Inc.
345 Hudson Street • New York, New York 10014

Text copyright © 2000 by Nancy Antle
Pictures copyright © 2000 by S. D. Schindler
Printed in the U.S.A.

1 3 5 7 9 10 8 6 4 2

Library of Congress Cataloging in Publication Data
Antle, Nancy.
Sam's Wild West Christmas/by Nancy Antle;
pictures by S. D. Schindler.—1st ed.
p.   cm.
Summary: On Christmas Eve, Sam and the members of his
Wild West Show help a trainful of people robbed by outlaws who
have just captured a very special holiday traveler in red.
ISBN 0-8037-2199-4
[1. Christmas—Fiction. 2. Santa Claus—Fiction. 3. Robbers and
outlaws—Fiction. 4. Wild west shows—Fiction.] I. Schindler, S. D., ill.
II. Title.
PZ7.A6294 Sac 2000
[Fic]—dc21   99-047057

The full-color art was prepared using ink and watercolor.

Reading Level 2.4

It was Christmas Eve.

Sam's Wild West Show was almost home.

Everyone was dashing through the snow

in sleighs pulled by horses.

Everyone but Sam.

Sam flew in his hot-air balloon.

The cowboys and cowgirls sang

Christmas songs as they traveled.

Bulldogger Bob played the harmonica.

Suddenly Sam put his hand to his ear.

"Hark!" he said.

"The herald angels sing,"

the cowboys and cowgirls sang.

"No! Shhh!" Sam said. "I hear crying."

Everyone listened.

"That sound is sadder than

a partridge without a pear tree,"

Rodeo Rosie sniffed.

They all hurried toward the sound.

They found a train

stopped on the tracks.

Sam tried to go inside.

But the door was stuck

tight with Christmas taffy.

"Help me pull," Sam said.

All the cowboys and cowgirls

got behind Sam and pulled.

The taffy stretched until—*BOING!*—

the door popped open.

Sam and the cowboys and cowgirls

fell in a heap in the snow.

The train conductor ran out.

"Help us!" he yelled. "We were

held up like a sprig of mistletoe!"

Everyone else from the train ran out

and started talking at once.

"They took our money!"

"They took our jewelry!"

"And they took our presents!"

a little girl sobbed.

"That makes me madder

than a bull that's just been branded,"

Rodeo Rosie said.

Sam was mad too. He saw red.

He saw green. Then he saw red again.

"Look," he said. "Wrapping paper."

Sam followed the trail of paper.

Rosie followed Sam.

The cowboys and cowgirls followed Rosie.

Sam stopped suddenly.

Everyone crashed into him.

"I have an idea," Sam said.

"Rosie, come with me.

The rest of you, put on the show

for these fine folks."

"Yippee!" all the children shouted.

Sam and Rosie followed the paper trail
to a house in the woods.
A sleigh was on the roof.
"Funny place to leave a sleigh,"
Sam said.

"And those horses hitched to it

are right funny-looking too,"

Rosie said.

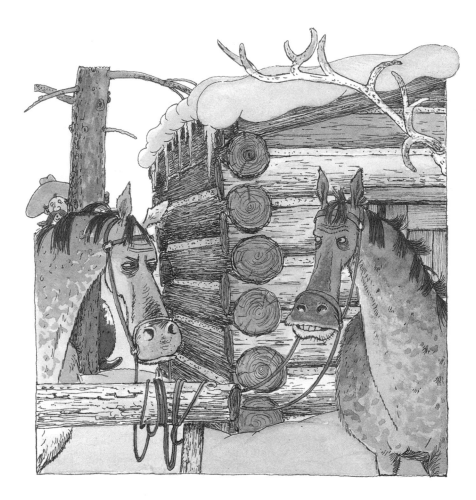

Near the front door

they found two more horses tied up.

Those horses were ugly.

They looked mean.

Sam peeked in the window.

He saw two ugly and mean-looking men.

"Flo and Bo," whispered Sam.

A very unmerry-looking gentleman

in a red suit was tied up on the floor.

"But you sent Flo and Bo to jail,"

Rosie whispered.

"They must have broken out," Sam said.

"You don't suppose they got those

striped pj's for Christmas?"

Rosie asked.

Sam shook his head.

"And that isn't just any gentleman

in a red suit," he said.

"I kind of figured that," Rosie said.

She pointed to the roof.

"And those aren't horses either, are they?"

Sam shook his head again.

"What now?" Rosie asked.

"Make lots of noise," Sam said.

Rosie started shooting

at a tall snowdrift in the yard.

Sam hid.

Bo and Flo ran outside.

"I'll be jingled," Bo said.

"She's making a snowman."

Flo just scowled.

21

While Flo and Bo watched Rosie,

Sam slipped inside the house.

He untied the gentleman in red.

"The Tyler twins used to live here,"

the man said. "I forgot they moved."

Sam and the man crept quietly

up to the roof.

The man got a big roll

of Christmas ribbon and took

two round things from his sleigh.

"Fruitcakes," the man said.

"They might come in handy."

Sam nodded.

Rosie was almost done shooting.

She put the last touches

on the snowman's face.

It looked just like Sam.

Flo's and Bo's eyes got wide.

They started to run. Then—

Whoosh, bam! Whoosh, bam!

The man in red bowled Flo and Bo over with the fruitcakes.

Sam lassoed them with Christmas ribbon.

He tied them up with fancy bows.

"This is perfect," Sam said.

"I was wondering what to give

the marshal for Christmas."

"Ho, ho, ho," the man in red laughed.

"Bah humbug," Flo and Bo said together.

Sam and Rosie and the man wrapped
the presents Flo and Bo had stolen.

Then Sam and Rosie took the presents

and the prisoners back to the train.

They arrived just as the Grand Finale

of Sam's Wild West Show

was about to begin.

The cowboys and cowgirls

were on their horses.

They all had candy canes in their teeth.

"Hey, Sam and Rosie are back!"

"They caught the outlaws!"

"And they found the presents!"

"Three cheers for Sam and Rosie
and the Wild West Show!"

"HURRAY! HURRAY! HURRAY!"

Sam tipped his hat and bowed.

"We have to hurry home now,"

he said.

"It's almost Christmas."

Flo and Bo were locked in the coal car.

The train chugged off.

Sam and Rosie climbed into Sam's balloon.

"We'll be home soon," Sam said.

"Faster than a speeding reindeer,"
Rosie agreed.

Everyone waved to Sam and Rosie.

"Merry Christmas!" they all shouted.

Then Sam's Wild West Show went
dashing through the snow again in
sleighs pulled by horscs.

And Sam and Rosie flew off
in the hot-air balloon to help a
man in a red suit who had gotten
a little behind in his work.